Politic...
A Rage Collection

Tara Campbell

Unlikely Books
www.UnlikelyStories.org
New Orleans, Louisiana

Thirteen Dollars US

ISBN 978-1-7337143-3-4

Library of Congress Control Number: 2020941197

PoliticalAF.net

Unlikely Books
www.UnlikelyStories.org
New Orleans, Louisiana

Political AF:
A Rage Collection

The Order in which They Appear

The meadow

The meadow considers the velvety slick on her skin, sips at its edges, trickles it into her pores, only a taste this time, she swears, until she falls in love once more with her own wet heft. The meadow umbers herself from the silken pool, plumps herself—besotted—against the dead, skin to skin, until she hates herself again. Eve shrieked and the meadow has hated herself ever since, has drawn the stain down deep inside, sworn never to drink again. She tries to make do with the blood of calving, of roadkill, of fallen chicks. But the meadow remembers the hiss of knife through skin, that lavish spill, that crimson burst of Abel. The meadow hums her thirst and hates herself, thinks *dynasty* and hates herself, murmurs *empire, infidel,* and *motherland* and hates herself because she knows. She hums her thirst and mumbles *tyranny*, whispers *homeland* and hates herself, trills *liberty* and waits. *Glory* she croons, *Halleleujah* she cries, and hates herself because she can almost taste it. The meadow sings *birthright* and hates herself, calls out *shall not be infringed* and hates herself and sings and sings and sings until she feels that velvety slickness on her skin, sips at its edges, trickles it into her pores, just one last time, she swears.

In the New Republic

we will call men "Sir"
or "Baby" or "Master,"
whichever they prefer
at the time.

In the New Republic
they'll only broadcast cat videos
and cooking shows
and Puppy Bowl
and The Bachelor
(never The Bachelorette)
and the Bachelors will put
all the women
they've ever wanted
into a row
and choose one of us
and choose her
and choose her
and choose her
until they tire of thrusting
their rose-red stems
into her
face.

In the New Republic
we won't ask for the truth
anymore
but they'll tell it to us
with a slap on the cheek
with their hands on our throats
with gleaming pistoled fists.
They'll say these New Truths
are self-evident

but we'll know they're not new.
They are ancient.

In the New Republic
sharp objects will not be allowed,
so we'll sit together
and knit our shrouds
with our hands.
We'll scrape wool stitches
over tender knuckles
onto yellow-blue arms,
and wonder exactly
which outrage
crazed the glass
whose blind eye
shattered the shield
between us
and the New Republic.

In the New Republic
we will have no choice but to knit
and whisper steel into each other's spines,
remind each other of the dreams we've
dripped into our daughters' ears. In
time they will know how to dig,
and where our bones lie, how
to slip through the dark,
and how to use stones
to quietly fracture
us, sharpen us
into the slicing
edge of a
jagged
New
Age.

Shut up and dribble

Shut up and dribble
Shut up and play
Shut up and stand for the anthem
Shut up and step out of the car
Shut up and put your hands behind your head
Shut up and bleed
Shut up about your wrongful death suit
Shut up about your rights

Shut up and take your mylar blanket
Shut up and get in the cage
Shut up and learn English
Shut up about where's your mommy
Shut up and change the other girl's diaper, and tell her to
Shut up about where's *her* mommy
Just shut up and eat your apple

And shut up and cook our food
while we lock up your children

Shut up about the Emoluments Clause
Shut up about family deals in China
Shut up and drink the water in Flint
Shut up and sit in the dark in Puerto Rico
Shut up about your crumbling schools, and
Shut up about the bullet-riddled children inside

Shut up about the Alt-Right
Shut up about neo-Nazis
Shut up about full-on Nazis
Shut up about Tiki torches
Shut up about the very fine people on both sides
Shut up about swastikas on headstones

Shut up about human rights
That upsets our new totalitarian allies

Shut up about Standing Rock
Shut up about your treaties
Shut up about your land
Shut up about coal dust in the rivers
Shut up about pipelines spilling oil out of their seams

Shut up about the factories that haven't reopened
Shut up about the coal mines that haven't reopened
Shut up about jobs that don't pay living wages
Shut up about jobs that have been automated
Shut up about jobs that haven't come back from overseas
Shut up about the middle class
The middle class is not a right

Shut up about your wedding cake
Shut up about your equal pay
Shut up about your birth control
Shut up about your preexisting conditions
Shut up about your baby's heart disease
Health insurance is not a right

Shut up about tax cuts
Shut up about budget cuts
Shut up about your Medicare
Shut up about your Medicaid
Shut up about your Social Security
You weren't supposed to notice when they go

Shut up about the shining city on the hill
Shut up about the Statue of Liberty (she's French anyway)
Shut up about the Melting Pot
Shut up about the American Experiment

Shut up about the American Dream
It's not for you

This dream isn't a wish your heart makes
but something you build
on stolen land
with your father's money
and the shreds of a tattered soul

So shut up about all that
because all I want to hear
is the thwock of a golf ball
and the fiddle
and the flames

Active 3D printer situation

Before you download
the plans for your AR-15
please also download
the plans for our son.

In case of loss
please reprint the following:
one son
who loves his dog
and his friends at school
and his little sister
and even his parents,
you know
he's still young enough
to say "I love you"
and give us a kiss
without blushing,
do you have the right
printer for that?

Please inform us
which resin you're using
because we need to know
you'll be able to reprint
his laugh
and reproduce
how he held his baby sister
brow furrowed
shoulders hunched
like he was balancing an egg
on top of a balloon.

Do you know the right setting
for how he always sat down
when he held her
because he was so afraid
of hurting a delicate thing?

If you have all of that
go ahead

but please also download
just one more thing:
this blueprint of an intact family
so you can recreate our life
before
just in case.

Showerbeer

But what good are words
when bombs spill out of your radio
every morning,
all your meals are gridlock
great bellyfulls of strife
with a side of extinction
shaved polar ice dessert
and a chemical warfare nightcap
with a tomahawk chaser.

You are a messy eater
you're filthy with grief
and sometimes all you can do
is take your beer with you
because water
can't wash everything.

Four-cent Father

Officers respond to a noise complaint
      black man playing music
Officers report
      in his own garage
"Black male, dreads, armed with a handgun"
      armed with dreads
who opened up
      black male dreads
then closed the door
      black dread armed
Officer leveled his weapon
      dread armed with a handgun
at the man behind the door
      "Shots fired, shots fired!"
Bullets splintered wood

Officers reported he had a gun
      found unloaded
in his hand
      in his back pocket
pointed at them
      with no trace of blood or tissue
he must have put it away
      before or after the shots
      to his gut
      and his groin
      and his head?

Jury responds to a wrongful death suit
      We can't reach a verdict
Judge responds to jury
      Keep trying
Jury responds to judge
      who asks for clarification

"If we find minimal negligence…"
      I don't understand
"…can the courts overrule…"
      Please clarify
"…monetary amounts …"
      Please clarify
"…presented by the jury?"
      Please clarify

Poet responds to a four-cent award
Please clarify
Please clarify how
Please clarify how a life is worth four cents

The jury finds
      one dollar to the mother
      for the funeral
upon preponderance of the evidence
      one dollar to each child
      for pain and suffering
      and loss of parental companionship
victim was under the influence
      no line on the worksheet
      for the fianceé
and to the question of negligence
      99% his own fault
      1% due to police
four dollars become four cents

Poet responds to the void
      Please
Drinking at home while black is expensive
      Please clarify
Listening to music at home while black is expensive
      Please clarify how
A stranger's itchy 9-1-1 finger while black is expensive

Please clarify how a life
If his taxes hadn't paid for the bullets
Please clarify how a life is worth
they'd probably charge his mother a fee
Please clarify how a life is worth four cents

One more question, your honor:
Did the nine-year-old girl
who saw bullets rip into
her father's garage
get justice?

Dedicated to Gregory Vaughn Hill, Jr.

The Trouble with Pronouns

"But that's exactly why—"

My lips and tongue freeze.
Another unarmed black man dead
and I want to be clear
but my pronouns are a mess because I'm
mixed-race
and
mixed-up
trying to explain
in black and white
how "we" and "they" might bridge the gap.

Why do my lips
sometimes lack the confidence

> (these lips, speaking out of a light-skinned,
> blue-eyed face; lips of a girl who grew up in a
> mainstream, middle class, two-parent home in
> Alaska, attended a multi-ethnic school and, hell,
> I'll spill it now, watched *Gilligan's Island* and *Get
> Smart*, wore *Hee Haw* overalls and played with
> Donny and Marie dolls; so how am I *even* black
> enough, because I have no history with collards
> or church, I don't feel like a caged bird singing, I
> actually *have* the bluest eye, and my dreams are not
> deferred, they are affirmatively actionable, so have I
> actually earned the right)

to say "we"?

But how could my tongue
insist upon meeting my teeth

      (this code-switching tongue, rolling out the right
      sounds by choice, by setting, by interlocutor; born
      in Alaska because that's the only place a black
      man could get a promotion in the 60's; trying to
      untangle *scholarships* from *reverse racism* in my
      classmates' comments (I did earn them—didn't
      I?); that one drop coursing through my veins a
      too-uncomfortable thought for certain boyfriends'
      mothers; spending too many years with rollers in
      my hair and relaxer in my regimen; smiling at the
      swaggy black coolness my nephew informs me
      we share; and how can I not fear for my brother,
      wearing darker skin than mine in a world where
      lawmen with guns don't hesitate)

to say "they"?

My lips and tongue freeze
and the debate rolls on
all mixed up
in black and white.

After the Pedestal

I get back in my car
and sit
crushed by the granite boot
of a Confederate soldier.
I was almost home when I hit another world
I had to stop
to make sure it was real

Welcome to Alexandria

I start the engine
glimpse rear-view mirror
imagine my light skin owned
a flash of blue eye heading
to my master's kitchen
or his bed

They fought for our way of life

Would my grandmother's
German immigrant bones
have ached for the man
she would never have known
but for the slavers' greed?

It's heritage, not hate

And yet I am here,
despite and because of,
my helixes twist
in a dance of violence and love

You can't outlaw history
        Ah, but this is anything but

You should try it sometime
come live out history
in the middle of town,
your head will spin
as you toe the edge
of the human race,
your keepers lionized

Try it, I insist
breathe through the impotent rage
you could only know
at the foot of the man
who would own you
pedestaled in glory for all to see

Because you're right,
history really does come alive
when we honor it like this

I pull into traffic
I know the way home
and it's far beyond this place

*The Confederate statue in this poem
was erected in Alexandria, VA in 1889,
positioned with its back to the North.
On June 2, 2020, after worldwide protests
sparked by the death of George Floyd,
the statue was removed.
As of July 15, 2020 the pedestal remains.*

Cauliflower

When cauliflower
gets curious it asks to touch
the tighter buds of broccoli's crown,
wonders if they would look as good in white.
When cauliflower gets restless it considers a tattoo
a little green band around its stalk or maybe just a
butterfly better yet henna, something exotic
but impermanent because who wants
to be stuck
that color
forever

American Beast

It enters on soft paws
and nuzzles your cheek
and tells you it's okay.
It says it's not your fault
your father lost his job
or is working three
or isn't there at all.

It prowls your house
and tickles your chin with Its whiskers
and says it's not your mother's fault
she's too tired to play with you.
Mommy has to sit, It purrs, and rub her feet
because her shifts are long
or her hours have been cut
or she hasn't had a raise in years.

It's because other people are willing, It says,
to come and work for less

It pads into your room at night.
It's hungry, but It assures you
it's not your fault the factory closed
and the jobs left the state, left the country.

Is it true, you ask,
that the jobs went all over the world?
It nods, and when you ask
who sent them away and why
It says, go to sleep
we won't feel hungry
when we're asleep.

It climbs into your bed
and curls up next to you
and tells you it's not your fault
the walls at your school are cracked
and the paint is peeling
and the water tastes funny
and your friend found mold on his sloppy joe bun.

When you ask why they don't fix the school
and the water
and the bread
It noses your shoulder
and says, but you had fun at recess, didn't you?
On the monkeybars?
It licks Its chops.
But did you see, It asks,
those other kids
getting free lunch?

It comes around often now,
rumbling in the voices of grownups
speaking softly after dinner
about the problems of the world.

It licks your hand
and purrs on your chest
and tells you not to be scared
of all the angry men with guns
who look like you,
because the angry men with guns
who don't look like you
are much more dangerous.

It's always hungry now.
It grunts and prowls.
teeth glinting in the dark.

But you're not afraid because
it's someone's else's fault
and when you get older
you'll stop them,
you'll pounce on everyone
who took away your country
and drag them all back
to feed the Beast,
and it won't even be your fault
when It chokes to death
on everything America lost.

The reek of history

The first drop of duplicity
fell on fetid clay
A worm stirred
A spray of hate-filled spittle
nudged a newt
In a drizzle of opinion
a toad twitched
A flash of virulence and the crack of rancor
sent a rodent wriggling
a lizard lunging
a salamander meandering
Torrents of abuse rained down and
drenched the sludge until it
stirred with the shadows
of all our original sins.

Bubbles churn up through the murk
burping sulfur
Grey-faced creatures
blunder to the loosening surface
The swamp gurgles and croaks
a fin slaps mud
claws rake dry land once again
The first one opens its beaky lips
croaks *wait and see*
A grunt, a snort, and the chorus
erupts in a corruption of song
up is down
left is right
lies are truth and
minds are closed for the season

A vole vaults into the cabinet

Are you wealthy enough for the age of ambrosia?
Hosanna in the highest tax bracket
Yea and a clown shall lead them
toward a pair of dice chuckling in a foreign hand

This reality is too much for TV, sweet-cheeks
We're fired on all counts, your honor,
in a courtroom just for us, because
punishment is for the ones who get caught
and the suckers
and the poor

Can we bail out of great-again?
Shall we grab our buckets and scoop for the next
        four score and twenty years ago
                is where we'll find ourselves again,
                    the golden age for grey-faced creatures—
            you didn't forget about them, did you?
Because they haven't forgotten about us
and everything they want to take back.

Now the bog is thinning
The swamp is draining, comrades;
it's draining into our homes
our bedrooms
our bathrooms
and hup, keep your feet dry in the stirrups,
it's draining into the clinic too

That stench is the reek of history
rising from the muck
where hatred lurked in the
sheltering slime
cloaked in civility
dormant in the dark

That's the stink of freedom, patriots:
the stench of the elderly without medicine
kids without lunches
queers without rights
immigrants without futures
con-men without consequences
Klansmen without fear
guns without limits
and fetal coffins floating like flower petals
o'er scum-filled waters

But we'll come to like it by the time it's up to our necks,
though we've lost sight of the children,
but they were much too expensive anyway

We like it this way, or else
And weren't we quaint back then
when we thought the demagogue would be
ashamed when that first lie
dripped from his lips

All Hail NewConstitution

And lo, upon the appointment of NewJustice
and the gerrymandering of NewCongress,
We, the Moral Authority, announce
the establishment of NewConstitution

Yea, and the wisest among thee shall learn it
for although according to OldConstitution
we cannot exactly require thee
to live by NewConstitution (yet),
verily shalt thou be judged by It
and by Us.

Which is to say by those of Us
who have been blessed
with a divine confluence of political
and spiritual Realignment
a great American movement
lifting up those of Us
who suffered eight long years
in the desert of civil society
and political correctness

Behold, then, NewConstitution:

Article 1
I am the Lord thy POTUS. Thou shalt have no other gods
before Me until 2024 at the latest. And if I can get the deal
Xi got in China, maybe longer still.

Article 2
No false idols. No graven images. No piñatas. No collusion.

Article 3
Thou shalt not tweet the name of the Lord thy POTUS in
vain, for the Lord will not hold him guiltless that taketh His
name in vain, and will ruin his failing business.

Article 4
Remember the Sabbath day, to keep it holy. Six days
shalt thou labor and do all thy work without union
representation, but the seventh day is the Sabbath of the
Lord thy POTUS, and all shall golf at Mar-a-Lago. No
exceptions.

Article 5
Honor thy POTUS and thy FLOTUS, for verily they love
all children of the world, regardless of any messaging on
the back of their jackets.

Article 6
Thou shalt not murder (potential exceptions for rage against
immigrants, gays, Muslims, Mexicans, Children of Ham,
those who don't conform to gender norms, anyone inside a
Planned Parenthood).

Article 7
Thou shalt not commit adultery unless thou art a celebrity,
in which case, they let thee do anything. In any case, thy
followers shall maintain that thou hast repented.

Article 8
Thou shalt not steal (elections, sweetheart deals for
POTUS family members, and Supreme Court appointments
excluded).

Article 9
Thou shalt not bear false witness against thy neighbor
(POTUS and staff excluded). Thou mayst, however,
conveniently forget the content of meetings with the
representatives of foreign governments under oath when
necessary for the protection of POTUS. Thou mayst also
"ad lib" without any consideration of veracity of statements
made during meetings with heads of state of neighboring
countries.

Article 10
Thou shalt not covet thy neighbor's house, thou shalt not
covet thy neighbor's wife, nor his manservant, nor his
maidservant, nor his ox, nor his ass, nor any thing that is
thy neighbor's. Thou shalt make a deal to acquire such
items at a value agreed upon by both parties. If the parties
cannot agree on a price, the richest of the two taketh all.

Article 11
The right of the people to keep and bear Arms, of whatever
kind, in whatever amount, and for whatever purpose, shall
not be infringed (exception: Children of Ham pack at their
own risk).

Hear, then, and abide by the NewConstitution.

And may POTUS bless NewAmerica!

A Growing Crisis:
A Presidential Address

My fellow Americans, tonight I'm █████████████ ████████ a growing humanitarian and security crisis ██████ ████████████

Every day, ███████████████████████████ ██████████████████████████████████████ ██████████████████████████ we have no way to ██████████████████████████████████████ ████████████ welcome millions of lawful immigrants who enrich our society and contribute to our nation, ████████████ ███████████████████████████

I strain public resources and drive down jobs and wages. Among those hardest hit are ████████ Americans and ████████ Americans.

██████████████████████████████████████ ████████████████ Every week, ████████ our citizens are killed by ██████████████████████████████████████ ██████ our ██████████████████████████████ ██████████████████████████████████████

██████████████████████ officers ████████████ ██████████████████████████████████████ ██████████████████████████████████████ ████████████ Over the years, thousands of Americans have been brutally killed ████████████████████ ████████ and thousands more lives will be lost ███████ ████████

This is a humanitarian crisis. A crisis of the heart, and a crisis of the soul. Last month, 20,000 migrant children were ███████████████████████████████████ ███████████████ used as human pawns by ███████████ ███████████████████████████████████ ███████████████████████████████████ ███████████████████████████ our broken system.

This is the tragic reality of ████████████████ ███████████████████████████████████ ██████████████████ My administration ████████ ███████████████████████████████████ ███████████████████████████████████ ███████ It's a tremendous problem.

Our proposal ████████████████████████████████ ███████████████████████████████████ ███████████████████████████████████ ████████████

███████████ from homeland security includes cutting ███ ███████████████████████████████████ ███████████████████████████████████ ███████████████████████████████ unlawful migration fueled by our very strong economy.

███████████████████████████████████ ███████████████████████████ Furthermore, we have asked Congress to close ████████████████████

██████████████████████████████ safe █ and humane ████████
████████████

███████████████████████████ border security, ██
██
██
██████████████ a concrete wall. █████████████ is absolutely
██
██

██ Vastly more than
the $5.7 billion we have requested from Congress. The wall
will also be ████████████████████████████████
████████████████████

██
██
██

█████████████████████ elected president.

██████████ Congress have refused to █████████████
██
████████████████████████████████ protect our
families and ██████████

████████████████████████████████ shut down █████████
██
█████████ My administration ███████████████████
██
██
████████████████████████

This situation could be solved ████████████
██
████████████ get this done. ████████████ rise above
partisan politics ██████████████████████

██████████████████████████████████████ why do
wealthy politicians ████████████████
███████████████████████████████████████ hate the
people on the outside ████████████████████
███ The only thing that is immoral is the politicians ███
██
████████████████████

America's heart broke ████████████████████
████████████████████ savagely murdered ████
██
██
██
████████████████████████████

In California, ████████████████████████
██
████████████████ In Georgia, ████████████████
██
████████████████ In Maryland, ████████████
████████████ in the United States ████████████
██
████████████████████████████████

██
████████████████████████████████ I have

held  weeping mothers and █████ stricken fathers. █████████

█████████ gripping their souls █████████ American blood █████ shed █████████

█████████
█████████
█████████
█████

To every member of Congress: ██ a █████████ crisis.
█████████
█████████

This is a choice between right and wrong, justice and injustice. This is about █████████ █ the American citizens █████. When I took the ████ office, I swore to protect █████████ what █ will always ████ help me ████

Thank you and good night.

Source material: NYT Transcript of The President's Speech on Immigration, January 8, 2019 (https://www.nytimes.com/2019/01/08/us/politics/ trump-speech-transcript.html)

42,000 Matches

Hate crimes are on the rise, especially against Latinos

You grab new leggings, skirts & more

Survival of the richest: the wealthy are plotting to leave us
    behind

You cook one-pan honey-garlic chicken & rice

Pardoned by Trump, Oregon ranchers ride home in style on
    Pence ally's private jet

You try the styling service that's transforming the way
    women shop

Sacha Baron Cohen fools Republicans into filming ad about
    arming toddlers

You put your pet's picture on socks. Free shipping!

Drought and drone reveal "once in a lifetime" signs of
    ancient man-made structures

You wonder, *How does this adorable necklace help save
bees?*

Trump says "DNC should be ashamed of themselves" for
    getting hacked

You watch as sneaky cat tries to take chicken drumstick
    from owner's plate

Plastic pollution has infested pristine Antarctic fjords

You clean literally anything you can fit in a sink with this
device

Cape Town 'Day Zero' drought odds tripled by climate
change

Your hydrating eye gel breaks through the competition

More mammals are becoming nocturnal to avoid humans

You're this close to the most comfortable sleep ever

Animals rule Chernobyl three decades after nuclear disaster

This food tray fits perfectly on the steering wheel of your
car

These birds of prey are deliberately setting forests on fire

Men build a world out of 42,000 matches just to watch it
burn

The Three sit and think red clouds. Backs hunched, they speak in cinders. They can only imagine what it must have been like to breathe.

The Three are hollowed out now: no lungs, no stomachs, no hearts. Impervious to hunger and sickness. They are neither male nor female, have no race or creed. They neither want nor need, designed to be completely impartial, untainted in their pursuit of justice. There were once more of them; now only the Three remain.

The Three sit on an eggshell stretching in all directions toward the horizon. The light falls flat and cold on their hairless skin, sun filtered through an ever-present haze. The Three squat on the eggshell, knowing it's tipped in someone's favor. Their task is to figure out whose.

"I cannot sit exactly where you sit," says one.

"I cannot see exactly what you see," says another.

"I cannot feel exactly what you feel," says the third.

They hunch on this curve, watching each other, searching for signs of advantage.

That one's back looks a little straighter, thinks one.

That one could recline if they wanted, thinks another.

That one could turn in any direction they chose, thinks the third.

But none of them move. None of them want to upset the balance.

The Three huddle and wonder who is better positioned. This is their final case. None of them hear the gunfire, or the laughter. None of them perceive the pop of the cork, or the clink of glasses or the shudder of machines boring out the core.

They only smell burnt oil and coal dust and gasoline. They know no other scent, but without lungs, they know they will not suffer. There is nowhere inside them for disease to grow. For them, there is no other law, no other history, no other justice. There is only the eggshell and the weak sun, and the doubt that they will ever find out who has the advantage.

And so they sit, backs hunched, and speak in cinders. The Three sit and think red clouds.

Inspired by a painting by Oliver Lee Jackson

Vessels of the State

we
will no longer
refuse you

we
will give birth
and give birth
to all required infants
from all of our partners
and all our assailants
and we will give birth
to whatever we can
from babies
to manna
to bibles
to frying pans
we will give birth
to world peace and war
we will give birth
to more
and more
and more

and we will give birth
to swarms of locusts
and shaggy red devils
with razor-sharp horns
and we will give birth
to dashing steel daggers
and gleaming new teeth
and we will give birth
to braziers and pitchforks
to praise you

for you we will grow
as many vaginas
as Kali has arms
our vulvas will steam
sulfuric, primordial,
deliver your mandates
and scald doctors' hands
with vesuvial pitch

we'll never stop birthing
and crossing state lines
dropping your children
like land mines
until tempests whirl
from sin-tainted chasms
and chains pour forth
from between our legs
to hold us down
and still
we will bear lava
and wait for our lovers
our husbands
our rapists
our fathers
our uncles
our brothers
we'll bear for them too
and praise them
and raise up new sons
and new vessels
just as you command of us
vessels of the state

U.S. Government Form BC-451:
Form to Procure Permission to Purchase
Birth Control

In accordance with the Maternal Priority Act of 2020, any and all requests for contraception must be approved by the U.S. Department of Health and Fetal Services. To that end, please complete the following questionnaire:

Name of Infernal Harlot (Last, First):

_____

Citizenship status
    1) U.S. Citizen
    2) Naturalized U.S. Citizen*
    3) Dual Citizen*
    4) Permanent Resident*
    5) Spanish-speaker*
    6) Olive-skinned*
    7) Otherwise suspicious*

* This is the incorrect form for your use. Please submit Form 4827: Voluntary Forfeiture of Citizenship Status and Form 3453: Requisition for Repatriation to Country of Ancestral Origin

Race/Ethnicity
    1) Caucasian or White
    2) African American or Black**
    3) Asian**
    4) Native Hawaiian or Other Pacific Islander**
    5) American Indian or Alaska Native**
    6) More than one**

** This is the incorrect form for your use. Please submit Form 3453: Requisition for Repatriation to Country of Ancestral Origin. Alternatively, submit Form 3423: Requisition for Federally-Funded Sterilization.

I, Infernal Harlot, (First name, Last name)

_____,
am requesting permission to purchase birth control for the following reason(s); check all that apply.

1) __ I choose not to have children at this time.
Please report for six-month Re-acculturation Training for self and husband. Be advised, failure to do so will result in a filing with your state's attorney general.

2) __ My family cannot afford to have additional children at this time.
Please be advised that per the Find A Way Act of 2020, the right of the child to be conceived supersedes any and all other potential concerns, such as present ability to feed, clothe, house, or protect current or future children. Potential parents are legally bound to procure such means should conception occur, and as such, all petitions for birth control lodged upon this basis will be rejected.

3) __ Bearing a child will disrupt completion of school/my ability to work.
Per the 2021 Patriot Mother Act, an approved and notarized Form 1426b: Justification for Continuance of Educational/Professional activities must be attached. Please note that applications filed under this justification will be investigated and may result in termination/expulsion from your educational program.

4) __ Health risks associated with pregnancy.
Per the 2022 Valiant Vessel Act, you must attach a
statement from your pastor attesting that the benefit
to the world of any potential child that might have
been conceived was considered coequally with the
value of its mother's survival. Please note, physicians'
statements are no longer considered valid.

5) __ I'm too young to have children.
Please consult the 2023 Budding Young Future
Act, which revised age of consent with parental
or assaulter's permission, and harmonized it with
appropriate childbearing age on a national level.

6) __ To regulate my periods.
Attach a statement from your husband along with form
HOLI-1: Certification of Training: Understanding God's
Plan for You. Please note, physicians' statements are no
longer considered valid.

7) __ Treatment for ovarian cysts, endometriosis,
or other health conditions unrelated to pregnancy
prevention.
Attach statements from your husband and your pastor,
along with form HOLI-1: Certification of Training:
Understanding God's Plan for You. Please note,
physicians' statements are no longer considered valid.

8) __ Risk of sexual assault.
Attach proof of address; most recent crime report
from your precinct, certified by a reliable male law
enforcement official; notarized letters from any
potential assailants granting you their permission to not
bear their children; and form HOLI-1: Certification of
Training: Understanding God's Plan for You.

Please note, all petitions based on reasons 1 through 8 will be rejected per the Fetal Host Act of 2024.

9) __ I am dating a married CEO or Member of Congress.
Attach copy of text messages and provide current mailing address below for immediate shipment of contraceptives.

Name and Social Security Number of Infernal Harlot (print)

Signature of responsible party

Relationship to Infernal Harlot (Husband/Father/GOP Elected Representative)

By signing this form, you acknowledge that you have given your wife/daughter/mistress permission to procure birth control, which may render your household subject to additional surveillance. Please be advised that per the Purity of Penetration Act of 2020, all carnal activity, including that between husband and wife, but with the exception noted in point 9 above, is purely for purposes of procreation. Anyone who knowingly commits fornication (sexual contact for purposes other than procreation, with the exception of point 9 above) may be subject to prosecution under federal law, potentially resulting in fines and/or jail time, and forfeiture of present and/or future rights to erectile dysfunction therapy.

The Scent of Lions

"Congratulations, Mrs. Costa," chirped the young Life Center nurse. "You're ready to go home! Here's your shield."

Maria raised the infant in her arms high enough for the nurse to slip the slim, silver band around her waist.

"Let's check the charge." The nurse stepped back and smiled, nodding for Maria to switch on her shield. Maria shifted little Leon to free up a hand, causing her bag to slip off her shoulder.

"Oops, you don't want to lose that," cautioned the nurse, looping the strap back in place. She'd just rattled off the contents of the WellBaby Bag to Maria a moment ago: a blanket and hat, formula (to be used only "if all else fails"), diapers, home vaccination kit, a full power infant shield, and an emergency replacement shield.

The nurse stepped back and pushed her pink infospecs up the bridge of her nose. "Okay, try again."

Maria slid a switch on the inside of her belt. She jumped slightly at the *fizz* of her shield activating—it had been over half a year since she'd last worn it—and little Leon's body stiffened against her. She rocked him gently to comfort him. As the shield quieted to a low hum, he settled back into the crook of her arm.

Maria stretched her other arm out to reacquaint herself with the shield. The field of charged particles followed the contours of her body, moving with her and extending about a foot all around her. She looked up at the nurse again and squinted. Maria used to see through her shield just fine every day on the way to work. Now she found it hard to concentrate on the young woman's face through the swirling, marbling effect.

"You're not imagining things," said the nurse. "Your shield strength is higher. We've given you an extra charge to make sure you and little—" The nurse hesitated, checking the display in her glasses. "—little Leon will get home safely. The shields in your bag have also been fully loaded."

"Thank you." Her voice was fuzzy and low. She cleared her throat, but she didn't know what to say next. After eight months, she couldn't wait to see Marco again and introduce him to his son. But the news reports: another aboveground school with an outdated structural shield, another angry young man with a tactical laser . . .

"Just double-checking your release paperwork," said the nurse. She paused, her eyes flicking back and forth behind her pink frames. "Your husband signed the Head of Family Covenant yesterday, so everything's in order. Is he coming to meet you?"

"He's at work." Even before Maria said it, she imagined the face the nurse would make. She hated that expression, the one that masqueraded as pity while it really asked why she had gotten pregnant if her husband couldn't even afford a day off work to bring her home from the Life Center. But to her surprise, the nurse's face softened.

"I know," the young woman said quietly. "It'll be the same with us." She ran a hand over her still-flat stomach and tightened her lips. "But you'll be fine." She adjusted her face into the official smile. "You'll be wonderful. Congratulations,

Mrs. Costa." The nurse pressed a button on the wall, and a airchair floated toward them. "Please have a seat."

The nurse steadied the chair, and Maria lowered herself into it. She took a big breath as the nurse guided the chair down the beige hallway toward the elevator. Leon began to squirm, and Maria realized that she'd been gripping his tiny body too tightly. She loosened her hold and kissed his head, drawing in his warm scent to steady herself.

Just fourteen blocks to home.

Life Center staff in pink or blue scrubs with matching infospecs bustled around her airchair, smiling at Leon in her arms. The nurse directed her into the floating elevator car and pressed the up button. As the elevator ascended the dozen levels to the surface, monitors in the doors ahead of her rotated colorful pictures of mothers and babies overlaid with advice for new mothers:

Do you have your home vaccination kit?

Download "Nursemaid Maia" from www.lifecenter. gov/infantcare *for voice-activated help.*

Electricity is life. For baby's sake, keep your shields charged.

Log on to www.lifecenter.gov/milestones *for baby's first Bible study.*

Golden Hours for September 12, 2056: 10:00 a.m.—12:00 p.m.

Maria checked the current time on the monitor: 9:59. Her discharge would coincide with that day's bonus surge in police drone coverage. Protection during the morning and evening commute was a given. The government had long since stopped the drop-in-the-ocean policy of holding Golden Hours after dark.

Once out of the elevator, the nurse steered Maria's airchair down a brightly lit hallway with powder blue walls and pink accents. They turned the corner to the discharge waiting room. Anxious spouses and partners lifted lined faces from their mobile devices; a few cocked sleek smartglasses onto their foreheads in anticipation of meeting their newest family members. Maria gazed past their disappointment. Nobody here was looking for her.

Fourteen blocks. With a full shield.

Her airchair floated past linen suits, polythene coveralls, and leather skirts, past shining high heels, scuffed sneakers, and thick, spiked jackboots that tapped out their wearers' nervous energy. She focused on the door, titanium coated with cheerful pink paint, rivets and seams all brushed the same color so as not to draw attention to their function as fortress. Above the door, letters scrolled across an electronic banner: *God Bless our Republic and its Mothers!*

She'd been out there, beyond those doors, every day before coming to the Life Center. She just had to trust in the shield, walk with the confidence of a full charge, and make herself the least vulnerable-looking target—with a two-day-old baby. Her throat tightened. She buried her nose in Leon's wispy dark curls.

The nurse stopped the airchair. "It's time."

Maria twisted her neck and stared dumbly at the young woman. She hadn't even wanted to come here, and now she couldn't get up from the chair.

"Mrs. Costa," prodded the nurse. "It's 10:03."

Maria's lips parted, but she could only nod. Her arms and legs were jelly. Where was the angry Maria who'd cursed herself for not having bribed the landlord to tamper with their apartment's septic hormone meters? *Why throw money away*, she and Marco had thought, there wasn't going to be any pregnancy for the State to detect. Contraception was the third highest line item on their household budget: after rent and electricity, before food.

And where was the feisty Maria who had struggled against the security forces when they'd come for her, who had fantasized about gouging out their eyes, stealing a laser, and breaking out of the vehicle on the way to the Life Center?

The nurse placed a hand on Maria's elbow and coaxed her up. Maria rose, swaying slightly as the nurse pushed the airchair toward the wall to await its next summons.

"Just remember, you have twenty seconds once the door opens to clear the Center's shield, okay?" The nurse squeezed Maria's arm. "You'll be all right."

The door slid open, and both women squinted in the natural light. Eight months after she'd been escorted into the Life Center, Maria hitched her WellBaby Bag onto her shoulder, kissed Leon's forehead, and walked out into the city.

Fourteen blocks.

Maria choked on her first breath of air. The inside of her nose burned. Her second breath pinched the back of her throat. She'd been spoiled the last eight months.

The door of the Life Center slid closed behind her with a dull, pneumatic thud.

Leon coughed, his tiny pink tongue curling behind the "o" of his lips. Maria pulled his blanket up over his face, but his tiny fist pulled it away. He coughed again and began to whine.

"Shh shh shh." She jiggled him in one arm and swung her bag forward onto her thigh, coaxing it open to search for a rag. Leon wriggled and fussed, and Maria winced with each rasping breath he drew. "Mommy's sorry, Leon. You'll get used to it."

A buzzer blared behind her, and she turned into the glare of a flashing red light. A mechanized voice informed her that she had fifteen seconds to leave the perimeter. She scooted quickly outside the white lines. Her brothers used to play chicken in their shields, and even at half power, they left some nasty burns. She could only imagine what a whole building's shield would do.

She fingered the bag's zipper open and found a thin, gauzy piece of fabric. No one talked directly about the air, but she guessed the cloth was intended as a filter. Sure enough, she found that the rag had a loop in its corner that fit around her neck, while the rest draped easily over Leon. She smiled at him through the transparent fabric.

She could do this. She would make this work.

The baby was agitated, squalling in fits and starts as though testing his lungs under the cloth. His intermittent cries drilled into Maria's ears as she tried to take in her surroundings. The day was relatively clear, the sun a fuzzy orb behind cottony, gray streaks. The street yawned before her, silent and empty. Tall brick buildings loomed on either side, half of them unshielded and boarded over. Down the road, the leaves of a lone oak dangled from spindly branches.

Maria made her way down the middle of the cracked concrete road, keeping an equal distance on both sides. It was slow going at first: her pelvis still ached, but no painkillers for her, of course. "Clean Mamas mean Safe Tatas." Only the female Life Center staffers would say that, though, and only in a cheerful whisper, with a little conspiratorial wink to make you feel better.

Two streets ahead, a pair of teenaged boys ambled around the corner, heads swiveling, eyes roaming. One was tall and thin, his head shaved. The shorter one had an inverse Mohawk, a single strip shorn down the middle of his light blond hair. Both of them wore their shields nihilistically at half power.

Maria slowed her steps. Stopping completely would signal fear.

With barely a glance, the boys turned and wandered up the street ahead of her. But just as she released her breath, the shorter one twisted and looked back over his shoulder. Maria was already getting used to the view through her shield, but she was too far away to read the eyes framed by the boy's twin curtains of hair.

The taller boy stopped and looked back as well. He didn't backtrack, but he looked Maria up and down.

Maria froze. She hoped money was all they were after.

Her heart thudded. Leon wailed, and she made a show of tending to him. Her head down, she kept her eyes on the boys, when what she really wanted to do was look up for a police drone. But she couldn't risk them thinking that she had any reason to worry, that her shield might have any weaknesses to exploit.

This wasn't the first time she'd been in this situation. She just had to be calm, patient, and watchful, like the zebras in the zoo. They were her favorite animals to visit as a child, before air pollution killed off the more delicate exhibits and budget cuts closed the rest. She would hold on to the railing and watch the zebras, their muscles twitching, nostrils flaring at the scent of lions prowling just outside their walls. She always yelled out to the zebras not to worry; the walls would keep them safe.

Maria didn't see any weapons hanging from the teenagers' shoulders, although attack lasers got smaller and smaller all the time. They could have anything tucked into their pockets, she supposed; the only question was whether boys like that could have gotten access to a handlaser powerful enough to penetrate her shield. She strained to decipher the low murmurs the two boys exchanged, but between Leon's cries and the blood pounding in her ears, it was impossible.

The tall boy finally shook his shaved head and walked away. The shorter one turned and followed him, leaving her trembling in their wake. She held Leon close and buried her nose in his smell.

Eleven more blocks to go.

She switched Leon from one arm to another and readjusted the cloth over him. His body curled with a fit of wet-sounding coughs. She wanted to walk faster, but the teenagers were still shuffling ahead of her. Should she turn and go down the next block? It wouldn't be as fast, but . . .

The boys crossed over the road and turned left at the next intersection. Maria picked up her pace, drifting to the opposite sidewalk as she hurried forward.

Leon's breathing had finally settled into a steady rattle. She had to get him home, out of this air. If he got sick . . . They could barely afford food and rent and electricity, and that was before she'd been sequestered at the Life Center for the past eight months—another bill they would have to pay now, despite insurance. That was the end of their nest egg toward an underground home of their own.

A cramp shot through her lower abdomen. She stopped and hunched over. As she rested, she glanced at a building next to her, hoping to catch a window for a reflection into the intersection ahead. All she saw was brick and a pried-off board, leading, no doubt, to one of the many "resorts" where almost anyone could still afford to slip in and get away from it all.

To ease the cramp she hummed one of the approved nursery rhymes, a technique the Life Center taught to soothe both baby and mother:

God Bless the Republic,

And God bless the mothers,
And God bless my baby sisters and brothers.
Mama will raise me independent and free
Because Mama loves the Republic and me.

She stood straight and walked again, humming as the pain subsided.

Ten more blocks.

Maria held Leon tighter, testing how quickly she could move without jostling him. She would have had him at home, if they let you; or in a hospital at the last minute, like in the stories her grandmother used to tell. No, she and Marco weren't ready, but she knew she would have kept the baby even without supervision. She remembered all the pictures from health class in school: greasy hair splayed across grimy sheets; steely, blood-caked instruments; blue faces with gaping white lips, a thick black stripe inserted over the eyes to preserve privacy. The price of disobeying God and Government.

She looked up toward the buzz of a drone, the blinking eye and sleek weaponry of the State here to protect her. Relief eased into her chest, and the thought that she was now only nine blocks away from home shot renewed energy through her limbs. Maria watched the drone whiz forward, patrolling the street.

Maria spotted another woman in the distance. The woman stood in the middle of the road, head tilted back to watch the drone cruise over her. As the drone disappeared into the distance, the woman began walking again, toward Maria. Maria angled off the sidewalk out toward the middle of the road again, still on alert, but feeling safer with another set of eyes watching out for her. Another voice to warn her of whatever she might miss. And she, of course, was doing the same for the other woman. "Your body, your responsibility," they'd always been taught. "And ladies, it's your job to look out for one another, too. Don't let each other down." Maria held up her part of the bargain, scanning the streets for both of them.

Halfway home! With just seven more blocks to go, Maria replayed her apartment code in her head, wondering if her fingers would still move automatically after so many months away.

As the woman got closer, Maria noted with a start how young she was. She was tall, and she had pinned her shining black hair up into a mature style, but she was just a girl, really; probably still in high school. There must have been something seriously wrong at home to send her out by herself. Or maybe she didn't even have a home anymore; maybe she was all on her own.

Maria's cheeks warmed with embarrassment over how much she'd worried about herself, being taken care of at the Life Center and having Marco to go home to. Here she was fretting about her husband working double-shifts for her and the baby when this poor girl was out wandering the streets all alone.

And rail thin. The girl was starving out here while Maria had bickered over the bounty of food at the Life Center, sometimes refusing to eat, incensed at the idea that every spoonful of soup or piece of fruit likely cost three times what it would have at home.

"Don't you worry about that," the nurses would tell her. "This is all subsidized."

Yes, but the subsidies didn't come close to paying the bills, she would tell them.

"There's an appeals process you can look into later," they would say. "Right now your job is to make sure your baby has everything he needs. Don't worry about the rest."

The doctors had threatened to put her on sedatives if she didn't get her stress level down. They may actually have done it at one point; she couldn't be sure. But she couldn't blame them, could she? They were only doing what was best for her baby.

Maria passed the young woman a couple of blocks from her street. She smiled and nodded at the girl. The girl nodded back and flashed a strained, closed-lip smile. Her eyes, constantly shifting and assessing, flickered only briefly toward Maria. Mother and child: the one thing she didn't have to watch out for.

Maria regretted that she didn't have any food or money to give her. But then again, there was the baby formula. Maria stopped and looked after the girl. The formula was nutritious, but would Maria offend her by offering? Plus, mothers were under strict orders not to barter or give away any of their babies' supplies. This had all been covered in depth in the Life Center's parenting classes.

Three more blocks.

Maria turned away and kept walking, ignoring the persistent dull ache in her pelvis.

God Bless the Republic,

And God bless the mothers . . .

She wondered where the girl was going. She herself would be home soon, safe. Marco would come home for a few hours before heading to his other job. She'd have to start looking for work again. State sanctioned positions for mothers were restricted, home-based and low-paid, but anything would help. Marco couldn't go on like this; he always looked exhausted in their holophone calls.

Despite everything, Maria felt a surge of hope when she turned the corner onto her street. There was her familiar red brick building, half a block down. Through the comforting glow of the building's shield—the same strength as the others around it, which had been a determining factor for their moving in—she could tell that most of its metallic shutters were rolled down. But one unit was home, taking advantage of Golden Hours to let in some light. That's what she would do when she got home: roll up the shutters, let in some light, and start planning for her future with Leon and Marco.

A sharp, female voice ricocheted through the empty blocks: "Stay back!"

Maria stopped. Was that the girl she'd passed on the street?

Laughter echoed, mocking, in response. The cackling was brash, male, predatory—and it came from more than one person.

Maria pressed herself against a wall and swallowed. They wouldn't have seen her, and her front door was just down the road.

"I've got a shield!" the girl shouted, but the boys just laughed again.

Maria looked up for a police drone. Nothing. Leon wriggled in her arms.

An electric crackle needled through the air—the sound of a shield about to fail.

"Uh-oh," one of the boys taunted.

Maria's stomach clenched. She could be at her door in thirty seconds. She could summon a drone from home.

Footsteps pounded down the street, first one set, then multiple. Maria saw a flash of dark-haired girl running past the intersection, followed by a blur of boys.

And then Maria found herself back in the street, running after the boys and yelling. She clutched Leon to her chest, his body tight with shock. "Stop!"

There were three boys up ahead, the two she'd seen before plus a new one. They threw their heads back over their shoulders as she shouted at them. Their gait stuttered.

Maria stumbled to a halt. She gasped at a sharp pain stabbing between her legs. Leon howled, his cries trilling with phlegm. She let go of his head to root through the open bag on her hip, spilling rags and formula to dig out the extra infant shield. She could throw it to the girl; but would it even help? She clutched it in her trembling fist and pressed Leon against her.

The boys stopped, waited, turned half toward her in postures of disbelief. The girl kept on running. Leon drew a breath, and for an instant, Maria heard the crackling of the girl's shield and the pounding of her feet as she disappeared around a corner.

The boys stood fifty feet away from Maria, still and staring.

What the hell was she doing? She'd run out here without thinking of her baby—or at all.

The short boy with the reverse Mohawk winced at Leon's piercing wails. The tall, bald one in the middle shook his head. His stare slid into a leer. He slipped a hand into a jacket pocket and stepped forward.

Maria stepped back, her foot crunching on a packet of formula. The short boy grabbed his friend's sleeve, saying something she couldn't make out over Leon's wailing. The tall boy shook the hand off his sleeve and stalked directly toward her. Maria's legs felt weak.

Trust in the shield.

The tall boy's pocket bulged; his fist clutched something inside. She stumbled backward, her feet tangling in one of the baby blankets she'd dropped. Leon shrilled. She should run. Why couldn't she run?

And why couldn't she see straight? The shadows of the boys loomed before her, faint blobs of color in a grainy, white fog. She couldn't move at all. Leon went abruptly quiet; his wriggling ceased.

"Remain calm, Mrs. Costa," a female voice intoned from above. "This is the Police."

She hadn't noticed the drone approaching. She tried to look up at it.

I'm safe, she told herself. *Leon's safe. This is a rescue.*

"Don't resist," ordered the drone. "You're in a stasis shield. You'll be safe while we investigate."

The blobs of color still lurked in front of her, unmoving. She could only hope they were in the same stasis she was.

Minutes of silence passed. Maria pushed down waves of panic, fighting the anxiety of being utterly paralyzed in the middle of the street. She couldn't even look down to check on Leon. She listened for his breathing, rattling but steady. She felt wet between her legs, and she hoped her hygiene pad would hold. She concentrated on Leon's breath, slowing her own, willing the throbbing in her pelvis and between her legs to disappear.

The drone's female voice finally asked Maria what had happened. Between gulps of air she told it everything: the walk home from the Life Center, the poor thin girl on her own, the failing shield, the three boys chasing her down the street. Her voice was shaking less by the end, but she couldn't move to wipe the tears rolling down her cheeks.

"All right, Mrs. Costa," the drone finally announced. "You're free to go."

Maria swayed as though she'd been dropped onto the pavement. She blinked the world back into focus. Leon sputtered. The boys were gone. Maria clutched her baby, spun around and ran all the way home.

The notification pinged onto her comm wall as soon as she entered the apartment. Within the minute it had taken her to dash to the door, fumble with the code, reactivate the building shield, and float the elevator up to her apartment, the notice had been served.

Maria rushed past the display, switched off her personal shield, dropped her WellBaby Bag to the floor, and pulled the infant air filter from around her neck. She rocked Leon, whispering to him that everything would be all right. She bobbed him on her shoulder, twisting side to side and patting his back. She laid him down only long enough to check her underwear—some clear discharge on the pad, a little blood, she'd consult Nursemaid Maia—and picked him up again. She needed his weight in her arms.

Leon settled into her body and she brushed her cheek against his warm little head. She rocked and soothed and breathed *it's okay now* into his ear until she began to believe it herself. Only after Leon fell asleep on her shoulder did she read the notice on her wall comm:

Citation (Warning)
Cited Party: *Maria Costa*
Civil Code: *Family Foundation*
Subsection: *Infant Care*
Charge: *Negligence—material aids*

Per Civil Code FF-IC 82.7653, parent is responsible for proper care and maintenance of all items related to childrearing. Failure to properly care for all material aids to childrearing (diapers, formula, shields, etc.) may result in a fine of up to $5,000 and/or 30 days in jail.

This citation is a warning, given extenuating circumstances. No penalty levied. Warning on record.

Touch screen to acknowledge receipt.

Maria scowled, and her face flushed. She turned her back to the wall and bobbed Leon. He squirmed and yawned. She gritted her teeth and calmed herself, swaying gently until he settled.

She read the citation a second time. No fines. No jail time. It said "circumstances"—they didn't specify what they were, but at least they noted them. The corner of her mouth pulled in resignation and she pressed her palm to the screen for scanning and identification.

Signed, Maria Costa

The citation swirled, curling itself into a tiny icon of an old-fashioned paper document. The icon split into two, depositing itself into antiquated file folder images representing both her records and the police database.

She was officially "on record."

Almost immediately, a notice from the Life Center popped up on her wall comm:

Dear Maria Costa,

Congratulations on your new family member.

We have received notification that you have lost/ damaged some of your infant care items on your way home. Please report to the Life Center tomorrow for a replacement WellBaby Bag and equipment care briefing. Golden Hours tomorrow are 14:00 to 16:00, so for your convenience, we have scheduled your appointment at 14:45. Failure to appear may lead to fines and notification to security services of noncompliance.

Yours in health,

Life Center, Northwest

Touch screen to acknowledge receipt.

Maria's lips parted. She blinked at the screen and took in a breath as if to speak, but in the end merely held her hand to the screen again. The message curled in on itself; copies tucked themselves neatly into her files and the vast records of the Life Center. She kept her hand on the comm wall, fingers splayed. For just a moment, she needed something to hold her up.

She wanted to put Leon to bed, change her pad, and eat something. But she should feed him first, and change his diaper—there was the changing table Marco had told her about, standing against the side wall. She had to check on food and diapers (did Marco get enough?), and she should start looking for a job. And she had to plug in the shields to recharge for tomorrow's trip to the Life Center.

She leaned against the wall and closed her eyes. What about the dark-haired girl; did she make it home? And what happened to the boys? She imagined the drone took them. She had to imagine that the drone took them, that they didn't escape and catch up with the girl. That she would be safe.

Leon gurgled and rustled against her shoulder. He was restless; he would wake up screaming soon. She unbuttoned her shirt and unclasped the cup of her nursing bra, then sank down the wall to sit on the floor. She cradled Leon and clenched her teeth as he worked away at her breast. She'd ask Nursemaid Maia about the pain if it lasted too long. She tried to hum a nursery rhyme to distract herself, one her mother used to sing:

Hey diddle diddle, the cat and the fiddle . . . the cow jumped over the moon . . .

How did it go? She could only remember the new songs.

Leon gummed down on Maria's nipple and she sucked in a breath. She slipped a finger into his mouth to readjust his attachment to her breast. She leaned against the wall, thinking about her trip home, about the girl, about how she'd felt running out into the street to help her, and the penalties she'd incurred. After a while Leon wriggled and cried, fed but now wet. Maria refastened her nursing bra and stood, holding his head to her cheek. She smiled and sang quietly as she fished through her WellBaby Bag:

God Bless the Republic,
And God bless the mothers,
And God bless my Mama for helping another.

Then a little louder as she crossed to the changing table:

Mama will raise me independent and free
Because . . .

She laid him on the table.

'Cause more than the Republic, Mama loves me.

Maria cleaned and changed Leon. Before she dressed him again, she looked down at his soft, plump little body. He clenched her thumb in his tiny fist and cooed up at her from his blanket. She leaned down to kiss him and breathed in his milky, powdery warmth.

"I'll do my best, little Leon," she whispered. "I promise." She scooped him to her chest and filled herself up with his scent.

In contradiction to the commander's standards and wishes

I base my poetry on science
in contradiction to the commander's standards and wishes
I sing of diverse transgender fetuses
write evidence-based verse
in praise of science-based wonders
rhyme "vulnerable" with "beautiful"
while capitol millionaires line their pockets
with non-chlorophyllic green
and almost forget to CHIP the children
in their trickle-down amnesia.

I base my poetry on science
in consideration with community standards and wishes
based on faith
in reason
in empathy
in data
in compassion
in knowledge
in questioning

in resistance.

Goddammit, you gotta vote because

when hate comes marching into town
it bashes streetlights left and right
incited by a raving clown.

They'll yank the phone- and powerlines down
to shock and choke us in the night
when hate comes marching into town.

We'll stand together—black, white, brown
queer, Muslim, Jew—against the blight
incited by a raving clown.

When angry men fling fists around
we'll arm the women (impolite!)
when hate comes marching into town,

and we'll sing loud enough to drown
them out, when they shout all their shite
incited by a raving clown.

But only votes retake the ground,
rebuild, and reignite the lights
when hate comes marching into town
incited by a raving clown.

Acknowledgments

Much love and thanks to the following publications for publishing the following works:

Poets Reading the News: The meadow, Four-cent Father, In the New Republic, Vessels of the State, In contradiction to the commander's standards and wishes

Writers Resist: Active 3-D printer situation, U.S. Government Form BC-451: Form to Procure Permission to Purchase Birth Control, Goddammit, you gotta vote because

Heavy Feather Review: American Beast, Shut up and dribble, A Growing Crisis

Quail Bell Magazine: Showerbeer, After the Pedestal

For Harriet/Shine: The Trouble with Pronouns

Rigorous: Cauliflower

FIVE:2:ONE: The reek of history

The Establishment: All Hail NewConstitution

Litbreak: 42,000 Matches

Procyon Science Fiction Anthology: The Scent of Lions

Escape Pod/Artemis Rising: The Scent of Lions (audio)

Unlikely Stories Mark V: SCOTUS 2247

About the Author

Tara Campbell (www.taracampbell.com) is a writer, teacher, and fiction editor at *Barrelhouse Magazine*. Prior publication credits include *SmokeLong Quarterly, Masters Review, Jellyfish Review, Booth, Strange Horizons*, and *Escape Pod/ Artemis Rising*. She's the author of a novel, *TreeVolution*, a hybrid fiction/poetry collection, *Circe's Bicycle*, and a short story collection, *Midnight at the Organporium*, which received a starred review from *Publishers Weekly*. Tara is a graduate of the American University MFA, a Kimbilio Fellow, and recipient of multiple awards from the DC Commission on the Arts and Humanities. Photo by Anna Dewitt Carson.

Other Titles by Tara Campbell

TreeVolution (Second Edition, 2019, originally Lillicat
Publishers)
Midnight at the Organporium (Aqueduct Books, 2019)
Circe's Bicycle (Lit Fest Press, 2018)

Recent Titles from Unlikely Books

The Deepest Part of Dark by Anne Elezabeth Pluto

Swimming Home by Kayla Rodney

Manything by dan raphael

Citizen Relent by Jeff Weddle

The Mercy of Traffic by Wendy Taylor Carlisle

Cantos Poesia by David E. Matthews

Left Hand Dharma: New and Selected Poems by Belinda Subraman

Apocalyptics by C. Derick Varn

Pachuco Skull with Sombrero: Los Angeles, 1970 by Lawrence Welsh

Monolith by Anne McMillen (Second Edition)

When Red Blood Cells Leak by Anne McMillen (Second Edition)

My Hands Were Clean by Tom Bradley (Second Edition)

anonymous gun. by Kurtice Kucheman (Second Edition)

Soy solo palabras but wish to be a city by Leon De la Rósa, illustrated by Gui.ra.ga7 (Second Edition)

Blue Rooms, Black Holes, White Lights by Belinda Subraman (Second Edition)

Scorpions by Joel Chace

Ghazals 1-59 and Other Poems by Sheila E. Murphy and Michelle Greenblatt

brain : storm by Michelle Greenblatt (Second Edition, originally anabasis Press)

My Hands Were Clean by Tom Bradley (Second Edition)

Made in the USA
Middletown, DE
28 July 2020